Perfect Endings

Perfect Endings

Elsa Lycias Joel

Ocean Books Pvt. Ltd.
ISO 9001:2008 Publishers

Published by
Ocean Books (P) Ltd.
4/19 Asaf Ali Road,
New Delhi-110 002 (INDIA)
e-mail: info@oceanbooks.in

ISBN 978-81-8430-326-1
Perfect Endings
by Elsa Lycias Joel

Edition
First, 2015

Price
₹ 200.00 (Rupees Two Hundred only)

Printed at
R-Tech Offset Printers, Delhi

I thank my children for they are the reason for these stories and Prem Bashani for his very being in my life. I can never thank my parents and brother enough.

Preface

My two daughters Lauren and Barbara are the reason for this book. As toddlers they wanted a new bedtime story every other night and our cupboard was already overflowing with children's books. So I had to create a new one every day and I did as another over enthusiastic mother. Most of them turned out entertaining and educative enough given my well- modulated voice and details. Some days the stories turned real as we planted a garden or went fishing and vice versa. Stories in the book aim at nurturing the good nature of every child, help them know facts and learn names, explore their tiny world through nature, prompt them to be a do-gooder and conveys the very idea of family bonding. Children imagine a lot and stories make imaginations rich. Capitalizing on the sensitive period of children when they have a strong interest and curiosity for nature is yet another motive behind this compilation of stories. Urban kids will sure take a stroll through imaginary and captivating scenarios of mountains, lakes, rivers, orchards, jungles and beautiful gardens as stories in this book feature a variety of information and perspectives that depict all things are bright and beautiful indeed. Our children may not get the privilege of living in a countryside so that they get to enjoy the ripple of a river, the blooming of flowers, glowing tiny creatures at night, the butterflies and dragonflies that inspire hope, singing of birds or a patch of land to grow their garden but parents should offer children the privilege of good books and read to them if need be. Also, with a little imagination, adventure and fun, this book of short stories will enable children sing their songs, dream and build their own new world in which there is accommodation, empathy, sympathy, harmony, healing and happiness. Not to mention Dr. Abdul Kalam at this juncture is near impossible, for he is one person who not only gets into the minds of children to excite their imagination but has an unflinching faith in goodness and deep kindness. When I decided to compile a few good stories, one quote of Dr. Kalam that played in my mind throughout was "Keep loving nature and care for it's being, and then you can see divinity all over".

Contents

Kalam Ji You Decorate India

You are clothed in
Nobility and integrity
You give each one of us
A reason to be proud of
Our nation that is to be
Mould and shaped by your dreams

Agni, prithvi and nag
Are your best equations
To take out the evils
And continue your journey
Towards an India
Hundred thousand miles away

You are a search light of hope
Beautifully sculpted by Him
To shine against the darkness
To show the way
Yes, you are sun-like
Leading light, oh yes!
Celestial fireball, of course!
A beacon, definitely!

Kalam Ji, you are delightfully our's
We hear you, We see you
We admire you, We follow you
That brings us spellbound
To the biggest factor
That's nothing but hard work

You are a bright start
In our adventure called
Developed India, thus
You tread sensitive zones
With relish, With honesty
Not with malice

From the small temple town
To reach the mansion of splendor
No opportunity you missed,
No hard work you spared
That's a feat you pulled off
By the virtue of your character

You very much embody
The mystic, enchanting and strength
Of a deliverer and conqueror
Magical elements grounded
In reality are you
Unique in every way.
"God had a dream before creation began."

□

A Living Goddess

The city was vibrant and lively. It was Nepal. There stood a palace, an old one. What impressed Martha was the giant statue of a monkey that stood at the palace entrance. She went near, had a look at it and walked past beautiful temples and open courtyards. Architectural masterpieces and palaces seemed to say stories of royal dynasties that rose and fell. She heard of destroyed temples and palaces that were rebuilt over the years. Martha was there with her hubby to have a look at the living goddess. "This is the Kumari Bahal," said Cornelius. It was an 18th-century building. Two large painted lions stood on each side of the door that opened to a courtyard. Beautifully carved windows captured Martha's attention. She stood enjoying the beauty of the three storeyed stucco façade. On the last window, Martha saw the beautiful face of a small girl with a third eye drawn in the middle of her forehead. Cornelius waved at the girl. The child glanced keenly and ran inside after giving away an innocent childish smile. That night Martha lay on her bed making a painful effort to come to terms with that little girl's childhood being locked inside a temple. Cornelius sensed Martha's anxiety and asked, "So, how did you enjoy your day?" Martha got up, "Good. But I think of that little girl in her mother's absence."

Cornelius chuckled and grinned and told her that the Kumari Goddess was a strong and bold ten-year old who belonged to the Newari Sakya community. Martha seemed to be enlightened by his reply and said, "Lord Buddha also belonged to Newari Sakya community."

"Yes, of course," said Cornelius, "I desire to tell you more about Kumari Goddess" and he continued. The girl is in the temple since she was four. During Indrajatra festival, the living deity in her beauty will move across the streets in a three-tiered chariot. Martha sipped basil tea and listened with rapt attention. After an hour Martha felt drowsy. She went up to the window. There was no wind. There was no passing shadow on the deep shade of the night. There was no noise. Martha heard the clock faintly striking 12. She went to bed thinking of the living deity and her life in Kumari Bahal.

The sun shone bright. The city was crowded and there was no space to move around. The king sat on his throne with 30 small girls standing in front of him. One girl named Meshwani stepped forward because her horoscope was consistent with that of the king's. Wise men of the king's court went up to the girl and said aloud, "Your majesty, this child has a turtle like neck, eyes of a deer, the eyelashes of a cow, soft arms and sparkling white teeth." The king commanded the girl to sing a song and he uttered, "she has the voice of a sparrow." Meshwani's happy parents took her home to prepare her for an ordeal that would test her courage. They forced her to sleep alone at night and made strange noises. Meshwani hugged her teddy and lay awake. At the strike of midnight, her aunts and uncles dressed up like demons danced in and around her room. Though she could not make out exactly what was happening, she remained composed. The next day, the girl was taken to Kumari Bahal. At midnight, the priests asked Meshwani to walk amidst buffalo and goat heads scattered around. Meshwani knew that if she screams, she won't enjoy the status of a goddess and her parents will be upset. So she gathered up her courage and with half an eye opened rushed through. And when demon-like masked dancers danced around with frightening noises, she thought herself to be an apprentice of Master Li of Jade Empire, a computer game she enjoyed playing with her brother. The king was told that Meshwani was fearless too. Then came the difficult task. The little girl was shown a decorated silver trunk with silk clothing and asked to pick out the clothes of her predecessor. Clues given by her loved ones ran across her mind. She crossed her fingers and identified the right clothes. The city came alive with joy and celebration. It was time for Meshwani to move to the temple of her living, the Kumari Bahal. Meshwani eagerly awaited the Indrajatra festival because she enjoyed being carried on a palanquin and then its her move to the outside world. From the three-tiered chariot, she glanced at her house and on seeing her parents her eyes filled with tears. Meshwani yearned to go back home. Alas! Her feet shall not touch the ground. Martha awoke from her dream. The sun was high and the broad day was clear and warm. She lay a little looking at the windows which were open and the curtains waving to and fro in the air. Martha spoke, "The day Meshwani attains puberty, she will be sent back to her family." Cornelius replied, "Yes, no doubt about it." From then on Martha prayed for the years to roll by fast and that the little girl would get back home as a sweet young lasso to enjoy life as yet another girl.

Martha and Cornelius reached home and told their children James and Kamala about Nepal and the most fascinating Kumari Bahal. Martha's son asked, "Did you like the Durbar Square?" I loved everything especially the lifestyle of Nepali people. Unlocking the bookcase Cornelius said, "Nepali people's life is centered around their faith on God and devotion for their religion." Kamala enjoyed the pictures of Taleju temple, Ashok Vinayak, Shiva Parvati temple, Durbar Square, Pashupatinath temple, the Buddhist Stupa of Bodhnath and other places of tourist attraction. They cherished everything about Nepal and the living goddess did charm them the most. Martha waited to celebrate Meshwani's home going.

"Beautiful people, beautiful places and beautiful memories."

□

A Night at the Lake

A few pelicans lived in a large lake. Every evening so many children visited the lake. A thin orphan girl named Jolly was one among them. Mama Pelican and her young ones looked lovely with their red-tipped beak. They swam, bathed and fished together. Jolly secretly wished to be one among the birds. "Hey Jolly, do you love this place?," asked a catfish. "Yes, I do," said Jolly. "And I don't wish to go back to the place where I stay." The catfish popped out again, "Jolly dear, you spend this night with us."

"That's a good idea," said the crocodile.

"Would you like to go across this big lake this moonlit night?"

"Oh sure," said Jolly. "Let me climb on your back."

Jolly patted the pelicans as she moved across the lake.

"There is a big white egg deep beneath the lake," joked the catfish. The drake laughed aloud. The pelican said, "Oh no, it's the shadow of the moon."

A coot called out, "Hey little on crocodile back, enjoy this night." The night birds looked at the pelican lake in wonder and flew around. The coot sang,

It's a joy to have Jolly
In our midst so early
She stays till the night
The moon shines so bright
She goes across the lake
Followed by a drake
And all her friends
Who are truly god send.

The crocodile dropped her on land. The pelicans formed a circle around Jolly and sang,

Jolly is our buddy
A sweet little girlie
She comes to our place
With a cheerful face.

"Its my big night," said Jolly and walked away happily.

The lake called, "Come live in my heart for I ask no rent."

□

A Panda Comes Home

James entered his house with an animal in his hand. "Take this Lauren," said James. Lauren moved away. "Grandpa I'm scared." Pearl took the animal in her hand and said, "It's as tiny as a mouse." Barbara came near, looked at it closely, "Pink skin and little fur. It's cute." Lauren stood away and asked, "Is it a baby of an animal?" James replied, "Come closer darling. Have a look at it." He removed his shoes, put them on the shoe stand and said, "It's a baby Panda."

"A female cub," said Pearl, "we shall call her Dipsy." Lauren moved little closer to Pearl and said, "Grandma, why did grandpa bring Dipsy home?" James laughed aloud and said, "Oh dear, Dipsy was left alone with no parents by her side. We must help her grow up." Lauren thought for a while and asked, "But what are we going to feed Dipsy?"

From the kitchen Pearl said "Milk."

"After she grows up we will feed her bamboo stems and bamboo leaves," said James washing his face. Lauren and Barbara loved Dipsy. Back from school the little girls played with Dipsy. The little cub played around the garden while the girls sang,

Dipsy loves daisies
And the colourful pansies
Papa brought her home
With love to Mom
Our sweet little Panda
She loves to eat dolma.

Pearl and James took care of Dipsy and she grew up into a beautiful Panda with dense fur. The little girls brought home their friends to show them Dipsy. "Wow! She is cute. Can I stroke her fur?," asked Tanisha. "Sure," said Lauren. "Oh, these bamboo leaves and stems! From where do you get these?," asked Young. "Forests," Barbara replied, "Bamboo forests." Lauren turned on the music and the girls started to dance. "Please reduce the volume," said Pearl. "Dipsy loves peace and quiet." Days passed and it was time for the girls to leave for their boarding school. They hugged Dipsy and sang,

Our dear Dipsy
We made you shaggy
You still look sweet
And always neat
We are going far away
We will come another day
To see you dance away
Hip Hip Hurray.

"You can tame the wild with love and care"

□

A Proud Watermelon

A watermelon lived among other fruits in a fruit shop. "I'm fleshy and juicy," said the watermelon. An orange hopped down. "Hey where is your pulp?," mocked the watermelon. An apple turned around and the melon said, "Your skin is red but not your flesh." The other fruits kept mum as the melon kept saying, "Guava is so dry, kiwis are sour, banana is skinny, strawberry is so small and so are jujubes." A small girl came singing, "Oranges and lemon, sold for a penny." The watermelon got angry and shouted, "But they aren't good for your tummy." Chickoos tried to hide behind bunch of grapes to escape the watermelon's comments.

By noon the sun shone bright. It was quite hot. A fat woman in a red gown walked into the fruit shop. The watermelon continued singing, "Prickly jackfruits and pineapples nobody wants to be pricked, pale lemons and sour mangoes, monkeys love you most." The woman took a custard apple in her hand and the watermelon laughed aloud saying, "custard apple, show her your seeds." It was sweaty and the woman ordered for a cup of cool watermelon juice. The shopkeeper cut open the watermelon and put chunks of its pulp into a juicer. Nobody heard its cry as the music was on.

"Pride goeth before destruction, and a haughty spirit before a fall."

□

Happiness is Living in Harmony

Rani was a bubbly little girl. She lived with her parents and was their pride. The people of her village thronged together for a temple festival. Everyone, irrespective of his or her religion, had a part in the festival. Little Rani invited her penfriend Niruba to join her. Niruba reached Rani's village along with her brother Kiruba. Everything about Rani's village amused Niruba and Kiruba. They just went along with Rani enjoying the beauty of the place. They felt they were in a different world. Rani's joy was overwhelming. She introduced Niruba and Kiruba to her neighbours and friends. Niruba was astonished to see people of different religion in their festive mood. The girls enjoyed the fireworks and sound of percussion instruments. Rani and Niruba decked up in their Monday best played around as elders sat in the beautifully decorated Pandhal. Now and then Rani ran inside the kitchen and fetched crunchy murukkus prepared by her grandmas and aunts. Rani ran and hopped along the streets distributing delicacies and tasting dishes prepared by neighbours. Niruba felt the pulse of people born to celebrate life and was taken aback to see decorated elephants for she has seen them only in zoos and during jungle safaris. After a sumptuous lunch, the little girls ran hand in hand towards the temple followed by Kiruba and Rani's dad. They dared the scorching sun and shut each other's ears to the deafening fireworks. By evening the girls' enthusiasm remained at its best as they sat looking at the caparisoned majestic elephants adorned with colourful parasols.

"Rani," said her dad, "I hope Niruba loved the Panchavadyam."

"What's that?," quipped Niruba. Rani laughed aloud and said, "The percussion ensemble." After sunset, the girls stood spellbound by the bright illumination. Million coloured stars illuminated the sky as the grand display of fireworks began. The festivities continued in the night and went well into the morning until the sun emerged.

Niruba returned home with vivid pictures of majestic Jumbos, fireworks, colourful lights and cheerful, loving people. Niruba reached out to her mom and hugged her. Up to this point of her life, Niruba didn't know that people belonging to different faiths could live together so happily because man-made tragedies in the name of religions and caste were so common in the city where she lived. And it was always considered risky to attend public celebrations. Fear of bomb blasts and terrorists terrified everyone. Children were not even allowed to play in the parks. Kidnappings and murders were a daily happening. Outings, fun and visiting hotels were a strict no-no. Niruba's dad worked with an intelligence agency and he always felt the city was unsafe. As kids it was difficult for Niruba and Kiruba to take this all in. They then got accustomed to a congested mechanic life.

Few days later, Niruba received a CD from Rani. She played it and squealed, "Come on mom, this is the festival." Niruba's parents sat amazed. The decorated pandal, caparisoned majestic Jumbos and fireworks excited them. Kiruba's pride was evident in his tone as he said, "I too was a part of it." In the kitchen, Mary arranged the rows of spices, jars and bottles. She said, "Niruba, we shall join Rani same time next year." Niruba walked up to Mary and said, "Sure mom." That night they enjoyed rice flavored with saffron and other spices combined with meat. And slept with sweet dreams of joining the revelry as a family.

"In all of our differences we must learn, learn to live in harmony."

□

A Story of a Hill

Gandhamardan was a beautiful hill with thousands of medicinal plants, numerous small streams and hundreds of perennial springs. In the middle of the hill range lived Chang and his big family in small wooden cottages. Chang was a skeletal 90-year old while his children, grandchildren, niece and nephews were quite strong enough to protect their living place from human predators. Barbara and her grandpa James planned to visit Gandhamardan hills as part of her science project. Chang's family greeted them. Barbara befriended Soubhag, a 10-year-old boy who knew every nook and corner of the hill. They spend time along streams, waterfalls and springs that made the hill look even richer. One day as they trekked along, Soubhag slipped and bruised his knee and elbows. Barbara opened her first-aid kit and Soubhag seemed terrified by the very look of band-aids and antiseptic lotions. He refused Barbara's help and came back with a bunch of leaves, squeezed the extract over his wounds. He said, "Here we have medicinal plants to treat almost all common ailments and wounds." Barbara questioned, "How about snake bites?"

with arched eyebrows. Soubhag nodded. With his help Barbara collected various specimens for her herbarium. Chang and his big family told James about people who destroy the hill's beauty in the name of bauxite mining. "Those people want us to leave this rich place," moaned Nibasa, an old man. Trees they fondly grew were felled to make roads from foothills to the top. But those little boys and girls never used the roads. They enjoyed the rugged path. Nibasa told James, "This is the piece of hill that dropped off while carried by Lord Hanuman." A little girl Nimba interrupted, "The other part of this hill brought Laxman back to life."

One night they heard blasts. Leaving aside their fire torches, few men followed James atop a ridge. James lighted his torch and he saw the crumbling down of a Garuda Stambha in front of a temple. To top it all a big stone went rumbling down towards the village on foothill.

James and Barbara left Gandhamardan. After a week, they came back with good plans and more people to fight against Bauxite miners along with Chang's big family. A few leaders supported the tribals. The felling of trees gradually stopped, there was an increase in the flow of the waterfalls, birds chirped, animals growled and howled, nature turned around its very best and they regained their paradise.

James and Barbara enjoyed a bath in a stream. Chang held James' hands and said, "Gandhamardan is our mother, father and God. It was our's. Now, it's yours too."

James winked at Barbara and they bade goodbye to those wonderful people who loved to protect and live on with nature.

"Don't let the greedy skin mother nature."

□

Barbara, Lauren and their Garden

Barbara loved purple. So, she also loved grapes, petunias, lilac and wisteria. Her little garden was heaven for butterflies that loved purple colour. Barbara's sister Lauren loved orange and red. So Barbara decided to have salvia, pat Austin and Gingersnap rose. "I love that verbena bonariensis," Lauren said, "Just because it towers beautifully over cannas and flax." Crimson curls 'coral bells' with helychrysum 'Limelight' added to the beauty. It was monsoon season. Their uncle Jethro was ready to help the little girls with their gardening. "Hey girls your plants will grow faster this season," Jethro said, "and I'll prune them later on." Jethro shifted potted plants to the verandah and portico. Barbara came near Jethro, pulled his ears to her mouth, "Why don't you shift the ferns and cactus to indoors?" He nodded his head and patted Barbara's shoulder.

Lauren sat idle. Her aunt Deepa asked, "Lauren, shall we remove raked leaves and pine needles?" Lauren did not answer. Deepa walked up to Lauren, "Darling, is something bothering you?"

"It is the rains," Lauren said. Deepa bent her head and pressed Lauren's chubby cheek against her own to say, "But why darling? You will see a brighter green covering after the rain." Lauren remained dull and said, "Water stagnates and mosquitoes are a problem. And many of my plants get damaged too." Deepa chuckled in reply "come on, we will clean our garden and make sure this monsoon will do only good." Together they removed cankered branches. Barbara overheard the conversation and moved to Lauren. Barbara took Lauren's hands in hers and said, "sister dear, this year Papa has promised us a beautiful and clean garden with a rainwater drainage in place." Lauren face brightened up and she smiled. Barbara and Lauren walked hand in hand pretty excited about the new drainage. They were very happy about excess water being drained away. The little girls sang and butterflies fluttered over their heads,

This bright monsoon
Our garden will bloom
Oak, chestnut and larch
Will have a good laugh
The rains are no pains
With good drains
We love this season
For good reasons
We wait for the rains
To come again and again.

The garden looked ready to welcome the rains. Jethro hugged the little girls "And how do you like it, girls?"

"Good," the girls chorused. By evening it was growing dark and foggy and beginning to rain too. The little girls cared nothing for this, being both wholly excited in the green growth and colourful blooms that awaited them.

Monsoon passed. The sun peeped out. Once again they were back in their garden. Jethro kept digging compost pits while Deepa pulled out the weeds from the lawn. Lauren said, "Uncle, what's a compost?" Jethro stood up, held her close and said, "compost is nothing but natural fertilizer for your plants." Barbara responded, "but compost smells bad." Jethro smiled and said, "but I'm building a good compost with weeds, vegetable scraps and grass clippings. And it is not going to smell bad." The girls looked on as Jethro continued to dig. Deepa walked up to Jethro with a basket of plant prunings and grass clippings. Pearl called out to the girls, "Come on little ones, let's visit the nearby nursery to buy a few rose saplings." And the girls went along with their grandma.

"Green fingers are a choice, a wise one."

□

Bears Love Honey

Bubbly was a brown grizzly bear. He loved honey. One day Bubbly saw honeycombs on an oak tree and his mouth watered. The big bad wolf always warned Bubbly in a scary tone, "Bees sting." Bubbly sat under the tree and thought for a while. Banta, the monkey jumped down, "Hey Bubbly, are you in deep thoughts?" Bubbly said in a low tone, "I love honey but honeybees sting." Bubbly and Banta sat down to think of an idea. In the afternoon, Shera the old lion roared, "Are you guys resting?" Banta chattered, "Bubbly loves honey but honeybees sting." They thought hard. It was evening when Hirna, the deer hopped by to bellow, "Hey guys, what's up? You look gloomy." Shera roared, "Bubbly loves honey but honey bees sting." It was almost dark and no good idea popped up. The animals left for their resting places leaving Bubbly behind. Bubbly kept awake and down flew Ullu, the friendly owl that hooted, "Bubbly, your skin is pretty tough and fur is very thick. Just take care of your eyelids and lips and reach for the honeycomb." Ullu reassured, "Don't be afraid of angry bees. Even as they keep swarming, you can sure have your fill." Bubbly got on to its feet clumsily and started climbing up the tree half heartedly. Ullu flew closer and whispered, "I have seen your friends enjoy honeycombs." And till next morning Bubbly enjoyed eating sticky honey, his tasty treat.

"It's a tasty treat only when you dare the risks."

□

Bunnies' Acts of Kindness

Once upon a time there lived two bunnies named Robby and Julian. They lived happily in a burrow and planted their own garden. There were plenty of carrots, radish, beetroot, cabbage, lettuce and spinach. The bunnies watered their plants every morning and evening. One day a crested mynah flew in to see what made the bunnies so happy. "Hi Robby, how do you do?," chirped the mynah. "I'm fine and so is Julian," said Robby and he continued burrowing away. The mynah was so tired after flying from one tree to another around the jungle in search of fruits. "You look tired and hungry," purred Julian. Robby hopped into his burrow and came out with almonds, "Take these almonds." But the hungry mynah flew away.

The bunnies decided to make the birds happy. So they planted trees that bore chikoo, figs, papaya, guava, cherries, pomegranate, custard apple and mulberry. Days and months passed. Down flew the crested mynah with her friends. They sat on the trees, ate fruits and sang songs. The garden turned out to be a lively place. Robby and Julian felt good listening to the songs of the birds.

Cute bunnies, playful bunnies
Our loving chummies
Good gardeners are they
Alongside friendly fay
Who helps bunnies all day
As they work and play

Creepers that bore strawberries and passion fruits entered the garden. Grape vines twined around scraggly bushes. More and more birds visited the bunnies. The garden was filled with songs and happiness.

"Every spring, summer and fall, seeds of happiness bore fruits."

□

Camping on an Island

Jethro, aged 15, was an adventurous boy. He and his dad James set off for a week on a camp to an island called St. George. They paddled canoes out to marshes and slept in tents. Few days later, Jethro's two best friends, Gethish and Jebin, joined them. And they moved to a two-room air-conditioned cabin. Jethro said excitedly, "Papa, this cabin has a full kitchen and a fire pit as well." "Hey Gethi, let's go fishing," said Jethro. Jebin stayed with James to help him cook and asked, "uncle, what did Jethro say about this place?" James said, "Oh, he just loves to be here." Jebin fried the fresh-caught crabs. The boys whistled as they stepped in with lot more fishes and crabs. James murmured, "Why so late?" Jethro jokingly said, "Papa, the gentle rocking of the boat lulled us to sleep." Gethish interrupted, "Yes, the water and the wind are so wonderful." Evenings were more fun. Jethro and his dad went cycling. Jebin and Gethi just strolled along oyster-shell footpaths and sometimes went picking seashells near the shore. "Let's slide down the rocky slope down the sandy beach," shouted Jebin. Gethi and a few other schoolboys joined him.

Nights were calm. The boys helped people stock campfires for the evening's meal. They came across drunken men. "Those men are muscle-bound," whispered Jethro. They walked further just listening to the waves hitting the sand and friends chatting around campfires. "Who are they?," asked Githesh pointing his finger at a group of sturdy men who sat in a circle. "Shhh," said Jethro, "They are night fishermen. They look drunk." James made the beds. The boys settled in and Jethro said in a feeble tone, "The noise around the camp dies down around 10." Gethish turned off the air conditioner, opened the windows and asked, "Can you smell the campfires?" James walked to the window, held Githesh close, "yeah, I can feel the cool breeze and hear the sound of lapping waves too."

Shortly after midnight, Jethro walked out to enjoy the stars. Jethro spoke softly, "My dad said he watched meteor showers as a boy." Gethish followed Jethro asking, "But did uncle ever make a wish?"

"Yeah, I suppose he did, with every shooting star," answered Jethro.

It was another fine morning. The camp buzzed with children. "Let's rent a Kayak," said James. They paddled out in the water and saw water birds swimming. "Children are fond of seashells," said James pointing to children picking seashells. Jethro turned to James, "Sure dad, They have a liking for the multicoloured sea glass too." Jebin and Gethi enjoyed watching the children splash water to tease one another.

The camp finally came to an end after a week of fishing, boating, para sailing and lot more fun. On their way back, Jebin said, "Our pockets are heavy with pieces of sea glass." James sighed, "And, I'm full of memories." Gethi interrupted, "What about next year?" Jebin put his arms around Gethi, "I made this wish with the first shooting star last night."

At home they talked of that summer's joy with a dozen of their friends.

"Love affairs with summer holidays never end."

□

Earth Day

April 22 is earth day. Little Barbie went out to tell her friends about Earth, our special place of living. "Good morning Barbie. What so special?," asked Shanaa. "Come along, I'm off to the park," said Barbie. Shajitha was on the swing. Shubi slided down cheerfully. Shami and Romola enjoyed playing on the seesaw.

"Dear friends, today is earth day," Barbie said loudly. "From today let us become friends of planet earth."

"What do we do?," asked Shanaa. "Little things. First, let us stop using plastic carry bags," said Barbie.

Second, "Do not waste water," smiled Barbie. Shami replied, "I always close taps properly and my dad repairs leaking ones."

Barbie and her friends did their best. One year passed. The very next year on 'earth day', Barbie and her friends came up with a new plan of planting saplings. "Let's water them daily," said Romola. "We promise," said her friends. The saplings grew up into shady trees and bushes. The brilliant small girls lived in a much cooler, green and beautiful earth.

Stewards of the earth are we
Nourish it for reasons so many
We are to create but not destroy
Protect this rich garden and enjoy
For a rainbow is a promise
And a sign of

□

Emperor

The dragonfly loved rains and rain dance. He lived in a beautiful garden beside a lake with his mother Queen and father King. A large maple tree, on which so many Monarch butterflies roosted, stood beside the lake. And Emperor's friend Damsel, the damselfly lived with her family near the lake. Emperor always put on a rain show flying up, down, backward, forward, just hovered and stopped while Willow Emerald almost never flew when it rained. On windy days, Emperor went out to play with Damsel. But she remained hidden because she wasn't as magnificent a flier as Emperor. Summer season began and Emperor complained as much as he can. Mother Queen comforted saying, "Rains will bring hoards of frogs and snakes and you go scared of the frogs' orchestra godoin-godoin." So, Emperor said goodbye to his parents and friend and set off in search of a rainy place. He flew and glided far far away. On his way Emperor met Wanderer, a monarch butterfly and enquired if he knew of a rainy place. So, Wanderer and Emperor flew together in search of rains. After a few months, they returned home tired and sat on a floating maple leaf in the lake. "Did you enjoy rains?," asked Damsel. In the middle of busy chatting, Emperor, Wanderer and Damsel saw ripples breaking up the mirror flat surface of the lake. Wanderer and Emperor knew it was raining. Wanderer and Damsel hid themselves under a leaf. Emperor swirled, twirled and whirled around in circles. His friends and family joined in the fun. Whenever lightening struck Wanderer and Damsel peeped out to see those awesome lights in the sky. After a while the rains stopped, the sun peeked out through the clouds and swarms of dragonflies, damselflies and butterflies showed up. And they took to the skies happily through a rainbow.

"Magical moments and colours emerge after rains."

□

A Visit to a Farm

Lauren, Barbara and their friends decided to have summer fun by visiting a farm. The day was fixed. Few of them wanted their parents to come along. Jishnu, the strongest in the group, said he would not mind carrying the snack bag. Sajan responded, "I shall bring yummy crispy french fries." Less talkative Joshua asked, "Are we going to a U-pick farm Joshua?" Nobody answered him. Lauren sensed that few other children didn't know what a 'U-pick farm' is. So she decided to brief her friends on it, even though they weren't visiting one. She began, "Well buddies, U-pick or Pick Your Own farm is where you can pick your own fruits or vegetables and pay for what you picked." Geona's eyes widened in excitement, "Lauren, every day we shall visit a U-pick farm!" Quite a few liked Geona's idea but few others wanted to visit an animal farm. Harshita stepped in to clear the air, "Hey Geona, there are no U-pick farms in Chennai." Lauren smiled with relief and Barbara chuckled as usual. Lauren, Barbara and Harshita knew that in a U-pick farm they have to pay for what they pick and it's not what they want to do on a summer outing. Geona was almost convinced about not visiting a U-pick farm. Sajan, Joshua and Jishnu were silent listeners. Aditya, another smart kid with bright and funny ideas, came running and whistling to join the group. With his trademark grin and raised eyebrows, he asked, "So, what are you all up to!" Jishnu came up, put his hands round Aditya's shoulders and told him their plans of visiting a farm. As if they planned Barbara, Harshita and Samyukta hummed 'Old Mcdonald had a farm' which was joined by Lauren and Geona. In a soft tone, Shiney doubtfully asked Aditya, "so, are we visiting an animal farm?" and Aditya nodded. Minutes later they all sat in a circle and Lauren said, "Now, it's time we understand the Do's and Don'ts" and every other child listened attentively as she said "Obey farm rules. Wear sturdy close-toed shoes, come dressed in clothes that you won't mind finding dirt or mud and bring your own water and snacks." There was a loud "Yaaaaaaaaaay" at the end of it all. Jishnu sounded doubtful about a fun and engaging trip. Barbara helped Jishnu shed his doubts. She told him that he could pat the animals, bottle feed baby lambs or goats that are grown there and hold baby chicks or ducklings. The ever energetic Aditya who walked past Barbara said, "I'll sure try my hand at milking a cow." By the time the children finished discussing it was time for lunch and Sajan ran home as fast as the wind screaming "I'm hungry, I'm hungry."

As days passed, ideas about the farm visit only got better and better with better suggestions from parents, aunts and uncles. The day arrived and children were all set with Jishnu carrying a larger than him snack bag. Sajan was munching dry fruits, Barbara turned up with her Barbie doll, Geona in a gorgeous frock, Shiney had a shiny scarf around her neck, a cow boy hat was on Aditya's head, Samyukta had her favourite Dalmatian fur bag, Harshita with her lovely little brother Sri Ruthran, Joshua with his naughty brother Jeremy and Lauren with a long checklist. Soon after Lauren was done with her checklist, the children boarded the tour van and off they went singing and howling and talking and dreaming of fun with the farm animals in the animal farm which was not so far away. At the farm Lauren fed grains to clucking hens, Barbara patted bleating goats, Geona learnt to waddle-like ducks, Jishnu was so fascinated by squeaking hamsters that snacked on potato chips, Harshita tried her hands at shearing a sheep, horses that neighed, snorted, nickered and sputtered scared little Jeremy and Sri Ruthran, Gobbling turkeys ran after Aditya who had a toy lizard and a salamander dangling from his hand, Joshua, Samyukta and Shiney petted meowing cats and Sajan milked a cow that never mooed.

Back home they shared all that they saw, observed and learnt with Radhika, Srinath, Prakurti, Tarunika and Vandana who were back from a summer vacation at Walt Disney World. Little did

Lauren and her friends knew those three were awaiting their turn day after day to share their experience at Walt Disney world.

"Old MacDonald's farm should have been noisy indeed."

□

Fireflies

It was summer vacation. Barbara decided to spend her summer holidays at her grandma's place. Like her grandma, Barbara too loved nature. Every morning before sun rise Pearl would come to Barbie's bedside and whisper, "Darling wake up, let us watch sun rise." Barbie and Pearl would go upstairs and enjoy the first golden ray of the sun. For Barbie the most wonderful thing after sunset was the sounds of insects, birds and the shining fireflies. Whenever Pearl wished to clean her meadow, Barbie would say, "Please do not destroy the meadow grass. Let the fireflies dance above it." Every night after dinner, Barbie would sit in the verandah and sing every time she saw a firefly dance,

You are my wonder
Tomorrow I'll let you wander
Spread your wings, fly up
And take to the summer sky
Be with me tonight
And spread your light.

When a firefly came to Barbie, she caught it and shut it in her jar. The next day Barbie let it go and waited for another firefly. She sang,

Here, there and everywhere
Light dance in the air
Please come to me
I'll let you see
Your friend in my jar
Twinkling like a star.

Summer days came to an end. Fireflies disappeared. When it was time for Barbie to leave grandma, Pearl hugged her "I'll wait till next summer."

"Fire flies are Portunes' will-o'-the-wisp."

□

Fishing and Fun

One day Prem and Lauren went fishing to a nearby lake. "Look at those pelicans dad," said Lauren, "they lust after every fish you catch." Prem nodded, "honey, may be those pelicans didn't find food for their young ones." Lauren decided to feed the Pelicans.

"Papa, let's throw away a few fishes to them."

"Oh yes darling. Do as you please," said Prem. Lauren threw dead fishes out into the waters. "Wow! They come flying to take the fishes." Lauren felt happy. With a twinkle in her eye, she threw out more fishes to the Pelicans. Minutes ticked away. So many ducks and drakes came quacking. Cranes, flamingos and kingfishers sat near the lake. Lauren squealed, "Papa we are surrounded by birds." Prem patted Lauren, "Darling, these birds eat fish." Lauren said, "Oh these beautiful flamingos! Look at their pink feathers and long legs." Lauren went around hopping and jumping. She was excited to see beautiful birds around her. She observed those flamingos and said, "Papa they eat seeds and snails." Prem smiled, "yes and sometimes prawns too." It was afternoon. Prem made fire and started to smoke fish. Lauren's terrier, Joe, barked at the birds for a while. Then Joe saw a chipmunk that scurried under a bush. Lauren laughed aloud, "Papa, Joe is digging to get at a chipmunk." Prem laughed, "Oh yeah, he thinks it to be a rat." They ate fish and watched Pelicans feeding on a turtle. Lauren put her hands around Prem's shoulders and said, "Papa, today I got to see pelicans' long orange beaks, throat pouch and big wings." Prem corrected, "A pelican's beak is called bill." It began to rain and they knew it was time to go home.

Next morning Lauren said, "Papa, we are going fishing. And that is that." Prem smiled at his little girl and started backing his boat out of the driveway. Lauren picked up their fishing gears and followed her dad for another day of fishing. Joe too followed them.

"Fishing is fun when it's simply sitting beside daddy for hours."

□

Flower Market

Barbara and Lauren visited a flower market. Janaki, a flower seller welcomed them. And so did the waft of the early morning scent. She sat cross-legged and her hands raced to quickly string marigolds and folded leaves of the Ashok tree. Winter roses, silky tulips and slender gladioli lay in bundles around her. Lauren and Barbara strolled along.

After a while Janaki called Lauren by her side, "Take these orchids, gerbera, carnation and anthurium." Before Barbara could ask some for her, Janaki gave her a small garland made of roses. "I want a bouquet," said Barbara. Janaki smiled and said, "Why just one? I'll give you two." Minutes later Barbara was given two bouquets of a beautiful mix of pink carnations, yellow gerbera and baby's breath.

"We should have a flower garden," said a beaming Lauren. Grandpa James and grandma Pearl loved the idea. Mani, their gardener helped them too. Months passed. Plants grew, buds appeared and flowers bloomed. The girls sang,

Asiatic lilies and oriental lilies

Dendrobium and cymbidium
Star chrysanthemum and anthurium
Carnations and spider orchids
Phenelopsis and daisies
Mokara and gerbera
Jasmines and bird of paradise
Gladioli, tulips and roses
Bring smiles to our faces
Flowers so colourful
Makes us feel wonderful.

Every evening Lauren and Barbara gifted Janaki a colourful bouquet. Janaki cherished it with love and admiration for the little flower girls.

"Flowers are colourful because rainbows are generous enough."

□

Friends of the Woods

At the beginning of winter, a small boy walked along a jungle. There was mist in the air. He carried a basket covered with a red cloth. Two hunters stood underneath a giant Redwood tree. "Where are you going?," One of them asked.

"Are you looking for somebody?"

"I'm going to see my friends," Sam said. "My mom sent me with food."

Sam looked terrified.

"Where are your friends and who are they?," asked a hunter.

"Birds," said Sam and he started to cry, holding the basket in his cold hands. Sam was afraid of guns the hunters had in their hands. So the hunters dropped down the guns. Sam climbed up on to a hill, waved the red satin cloth in the air and called out "Here I am, Sam, with fruits and nuts. Fly down and have your fill." And from every direction flew down birds of bright colours. A cuckoo and a sparrow perched on Sam's shoulders. There were parrots, macaws, tailor birds, weaver birds, herons, flamingos, eagles, vultures, pigeons, cranes, peahens, peacocks, pheasants and lot more. The jungle was no more silent and scary. The chirping of happy birds and Sam's voice filled the air. After an hour it began to snow. The birds flew away and Sam climbed down the hill. The hunters were surprised. They asked Sam, "How did you make friends with these wild birds?" Sam was no longer scared. He looked into their eyes and said, "I just don't harm them and they know it."

"Aren't you scared of wild animals?," asked a hunter.

Sam replied with a smile, "Yes I do. But they live deep inside. And most of them sleep during winter."

From then on those hunters no longer wanted to be hunters. Every winter they went along with Sam to feed those birds in the jungle.

"Hunting animals for the thrill of it is brutality." □

Gardening is Fun

Margaret and Stephens lived in a beautiful cottage with their grandchildren Pearl, Priya, Ruby, Sam, Judy, Julian, Robert, Vimla, Viji, Vinu, Vince, Nithya and Jane.

"Gramma, what are you doing?," asked Pearl seeing her grandma walk into the front yard with a pickaxe in hand. Margaret remained silent. Pearl came closer and saw her remove the wilting seed-heads from Rhododendrons. "Gramma, I think you can do the same with Azaleas too," said Pearl. Margaret looked over her shoulders, smiled and continued her job. Pearl went off to remove sucker growths from her favourite mango tree.

Ruby loved roses and took care of the rose plants. So, she strutted towards the rose garden with a pesticide spray. Stephens followed ruby saying, "Take care, Pesticides are poisonous." He questioned, "Are you spraying for Aphids?" Ruby nodded. Nithya pointed out black spot and said, "These are bad for the roses."

Just then, Ruby cried out, "Here is a rose-chafer feeding on my yellow rose." Margaret walked across to the rose garden. Pearl came running to see what a rose chafer looked like. "Wow!," exclaimed Pearl, " A beautiful shiny yellow beetle." Jane took it in her hands for a closer look. Priya slid behind Pearl. After a few seconds, it flew away.

Julian pruned Forsythias, Weigela and Spiraea. Robert helped him with a pruning hook. "Thanks a lot Robert. The work is almost done," said Julian. Robert walked away saying, "Those lilacs have finished blooming and its time to prune them too."

Margaret called out "kiddos remove the lawn weeds." Vimla questioned "By hand-pulling?" Stephens said, "Of course darling. The mower is under repair." Margaret's pet dog Tiger came with a hatchet in its mouth to join the children. It handed over the hatchet to Stephens and he started to cut the branches of the oldest-canes.

Vinu cried out, "Granny look here, there are slugs and snails. Oh my God! They will devastate our garden." Margaret came closer to the children to assure them, "There are not so much of them. We'll remove them."

Judy, Jane and Viji enjoyed watching the butterflies that fluttered around the magnolia in its full bloom. Vince and Viji planted a few peonies because they loved pink.

The children happily pulled out weeds singing:

This is our garden
With pansies and snapdragons
Granny loves Fuchsias
Grandpa loves Petunias

Geraniums and Impatiens
Our imagination and fascination
We feel so good
About salvia and Marigolds
Zinnias and Lobelia
Invite colourful butterflies
Flower peckers and honeyeaters
And a few dragonflies
To add beauty
To our flower-bed
Hydrangeas and Bougainvillea
Daisies and poppies
Larkspurs and marigolds
Their smiles unfold
Roses and bellflowers
Our favourite flowerers
Gladioli and tulips
Shake their hips
They dance in the breeze
In our playground of fairies.

Around noon they heard thunder and saw lightning cut across the skies. All of a sudden the clouds opened. "Kiddos rush inside," shouted Stephens. They sat on the verandah to enjoy their garden. Pearl leaned on to Margaret and said, "It's a kaleidoscope of colours." Margaret held Pearl closer and watched with wonder their garden of flowers, shrubs and trees.

"Nature has the most colourful and beautiful smile."

□

Hridey

On a drowsy summer morning, Barbara went to meet her friend Hridey who lived in a village. The village people dressed smart and walked briskly. Barbara heard birds chirping and children playing in a distance. She kept walking and a small boy zipping by on a bicycle greeted her, "Good morning girlie. You are Hridey's friend, I suppose." Barbara smiled back and nodded her head. Barbara asked him for direction to Hridey's house and she knew she was only a few meters from it. Barbara had walked a long distance. So, she decided to rest under the sprawling shady trees on a playground. She watched happy children playing kho-kho and a few other kids racing each other up and down the ground. Amidst all this, she noticed something very unusual about the village. There were about 30 similar houses, all painted in shades of pink. Barbara spotted a small boy pulling out weeds from his small garden outside his house. Barbara walked up to him, "Hi, I'm Barbara, Hridey's friend," the little boy looked up and gave away a smile, "I'm Ritesh." Soon they were chatting as if they knew each other well. Ritesh told Barbara that Hridey was brilliant, full of energy and always talked about his dreams. A lady came out of the house and so many children followed her. "Amma, is she our guest?" a little girl asked the lady. They all sat for a friendly chat. Barbara understood she has reached an orphanage with special people. Each house had a caretaker, who the orphaned children addressed as 'Amma'. Hridey lived in one of those houses. As the kids spoke to Barbara, she thought of the sense of belonging and happiness Hridey exhibited at school. And how lovingly he spoke of his amma and siblings! Barbara just couldn't comprehend as to how strangers with different backgrounds could end up in a place as mother and children. She was very clear that the brothers and sisters of that small village weren't born in a single home. The day turned to evening and Hridey was by Barbara's side telling her about his eldest sister who used to visit him with her small daughter. Hridey sang his all time favourite song for Barbara when it was time for her to leave:

We are little children
who love to have fun
be at school or home
we are never alone

parents our mentors
brothers and sisters
friends and cousins
never unbinding

we are always loved
to our family we bow
with gratitude and respect
for giving us life's best

our dreams are a myriad
cared for and shared
and we reach for the stars
really really fast.

That day Barbara understood the power of love. Back at home Barbara told her grandma, "This is Hridey's time for dinner." Pearl replied, "Yes darling, this world has people who deserve a home more than anything. And God knows it."

"Homes are built on love and trust."

□

Jungle Jingle

It was a fine warm day in the jungle. The lion roared, "Dear friends, what do we do today?" The bunny came hopping, "Your majesty, we shall fly kites." The grizzly bear grunted, "But the day is not windy." Three of them sat under a shady gulmohar tree. The lion looked up and saw a happy little monkey swinging on the branches. He leapt from one branch to the other. "Hey monkey, will you please come join us?" woofed the grizzly bear. And the monkey came down and shared the peanuts he had with the lion, bear and bunny. "I don't eat peanuts," roared the lion. "And so do I," honked the bunny. The monkey thought for a while and chattered, "Shall we go boating?" Just then the two kangaroos Winnie and Minnie who row the boat joined them. "Why do you look so tired, Minnie?," rumbled the lion. "Last night Minnie caught a cold and today morning she is down with fever," grumbled a sad Winnie. The animals kept silent thinking of different ways to make their day.

Hey it's a warm day
A beautiful sunny day
The sun shines brightly

To make us happy
This is our jungle
Our only place to jingle.

Chirped a brightly coloured Macaw. Soon, so many sparrows, cuckoos, robins, kingfishers and parrots joined the Macaw.

Far away the animals saw the old elephant walking towards them. The elephant was wise and always came up with bright ideas. "Dear Jumbo, tell us an idea to spend this day," roared the lion. The proud elephant trumpeted, "Let's sing songs." The animals too didn't want to leave sick Minnie alone. And they all gathered near a big calm lake. A tiger, porcupine, giraffe, zebra, rhinoceros, hippopotamus, bison, wolf, deer and cheetah joined them. The lion requested the fox to sing a song. The fox howled aloud.

I'm the fox
As big as the dogs
I'm very cunning
Always naughty and hunting
I hunt the chicks
The hens and ducks
I scare them away
And keep them at bay.

The giraffe strutted across

I'm the tallest
But not the cutest

Long neck is my asset
Why would I fret?
I can reach for any tree
Especially the acacia tree
My tongue is bluish purple
I never chew on a 'Center Fruit'.

The song made the animals laugh. In the afternoon, monkey prepared a powder made of pepper, dried ginger and neem leaves and screeched "Minnie eat a teaspoon of this." Minnie ate it and she started to sneeze and cough. Once again the animals sang

Minnie caught a cold
And couldn't row a boat
She is down with fever
So monkey bought some pepper
Minnie feels quite better
She asks for bread and butter
Winnie hops away faster
To the nearby baker.

As every animal sang a song, the ostrich and meerkat danced along making the animals happy. By evening Minnie felt better. "Thank you good friends for making my day," grunted Minnie. The elephant walked away trumpeting, "Today was wonderful." The sun set, promising to rise again.

"Nothing can replace a Jungle choir."

□

Kitty and Betty

Kitty, the kitten loved traveling. "I'm off to find cool and charming places," meowed Kitty to her mom Rosy.

"Good. Its hot here. Take care," chirred Rosy. Kitty set off. She walked, walked and walked.

"Good morning Kitty, where are you going?," purred Betty.

"Betty dear, I'm going to some cool and beautiful place," meowed Kitty. Betty joined Kitty. Together they went walking. They reached the deep forests. The sky turned cloudy. "It's drizzling," growled Kitty. "Oh yes buddy! that's nice. I can hear bird and animal calls," chirred Betty. "And the smell of bamboo and teak," hissed Kitty. They saw tigers, lions, elephants, deers, wild boars and bears. "Look, they all run for shelter," meowed Kitty. Betty nodded, "Yes, it rains heavily." The weather turned cold. A bunny sat safe inside his burrow. Kitty Chirred, "dear Mr. Bunny, may we come inside?"

"Oh sure," wheeked the bunny.

The kittens hopped into the burrow. When the rain stopped Betty purred, "The weather is pleasant." "Can you hear the water dripping off the leaves?," futtered the bunny. The sun slowly spread its golden rays. The bunny hopped out of his burrow and wheeked, "let's enjoy the mild sun and breathe in the cool air." All the animals came out. The elephant danced and the cuckoo sang:

Deep in the jungle
Jumbo does a jingle
With his friends so many
Cheered by the bunny.

Kitty and Betty started walking again. They walked, hopped and ran across mountains, around lakes and twisting roads. They stopped by a park. "Let us relax," Kitty sat on a bench. Betty climbed up a tree. The kittens enjoyed the music in the park. Children played around. "Look Betty, the kids are sucking iced candy," meowed Kitty.

They reached a river flowing past. "Let's rest here on this river bank," yowled a tired Kitty. Betty howled, "I'm hungry too." Just then Kitty screeched, "Look betty dear, I've found tasty pieces of chicken." They ate chicken. Soon it became night. "We shall sleep under this neem tree," yawned and stretched Betty. They slept. After a few minutes, Betty woke up, "I hear the sound of pounding hooves." Scratching her head, Kitty purred, "I too. It may be wild boars." The kitten went back to sleep. Next morning, the sun shone bright. "Let's go home," meowed Kitty and the kittens started their journey back home. They sang:

We cross fields and mountains

We see fishes in a fountain
And walk along the zoo
We say 'hello' to the kangaroo.

"Hey Kitty, you are back home," chirred Rosy. "How was your trip?," hissed Craig the jealous cat.

"Lambs, goats, pigs, chicken and sheep, come along and listen to our story," screeched Betty.

They sat under a shady banyan tree. Kitty began:

One two three
We went on a journey
Across mountains, lakes and rivers
And jungles so warmer
Jumbo did a cha-cha-cha
Monkeys did a salsa
We saw lovely gardens
Watered by pretty maidens
We stopped to smell roses
We jumped into a zoo
To meet a kangaroo
Betty hugged his long neck
I gave him a peck.

At night, everyone went to sleep. Next morning the lambs, goats, pigs, chicken and sheep lined up under the banyan tree. "Another story telling day," meowed Betty as she.

"Animals too have enough reasons to have some fun."

□

Little Girls Spot Fairies

◇◇◇

Lauren lived with her grandma Pearl in a beautiful cottage. Lauren loved lilies and so Pearl had lots of lilies in her colourful garden. Lauren and Pearl enjoyed watering the plants. One night after bedtime stories, Lauren questioned, "Are fairies born in flowers?" Grandma nodded with a smile, "They are also born in the first smile of a baby." Lauren thought for a while, yawned and sat up, "grandma, will I ever get to see one in our garden?" Pearl tucked her in, "Of course honey, you will get to see so many someday."

The clock struck twelve and Lauren stood in her grandma's garden. Slowly and steadily, she tiptoed towards the Easter lily. "WOW," she whispered for there curled up a beautiful small fairy dressed in petals inside the flower. Lauren was too careful about not making a noise because she knew flower fairies are shy and if they see her they would disappear. She slowly moved to a Trumpet lily and spotted another beautiful fairy. Turk's cap lily had an adoring one, Madonna lily had a charming one, Leapord lily had a cute one and Stargazer had a gorgeous one gazing at the stars. Lauren thought to herself, "yes, flower fairies love music and dancing." Lauren sang:

Are you the wild cherry?
Who makes me merry!
Are you the Almond Blossom?
You are nothing but awesome!
Are you the Lavender?
Let's twirl around in wonder!
Are you my gentle Rose?
Let me come close
Are you pretty Zinnia?
Everyone's friend and diva!
There is my Buttercup!
Oh my gosh! You are all up!
Now grant me my wishes
And your sweet kisses
Before you go away
To dance, glide, sing and play.

Before Lauren could make her wishes, she felt Pearl's gentle touch. "Wake up darling, it's already Eight 'O-clock." Lovely Lauren hugged her grandma "Oh nanny, how I wish my dream came true!" And Lauren clapped her hands till she grew tired because she believed in fairies.

"Fairies are stewards of goodness."

□

Love Came Back

Liza was born into a loving family. She lived in a remote land far away from the bustling city. She was in the third standard and her class teacher Sugirtha loved her so much that after school time the teacher had a word or two with the small girl. The little girl's legs would bounce up and down with excitement. Not all of Liza's family members were well educated except her aunt Martha who was a doctor. Martha never wished to make big money. So, she stayed back in her village to help people live a healthy life. During holidays, Liza and Martha would spend time watching birds. "Mourning doves," said Liza. One morning they came across thousands of doves on a steep cliff near a barley field. Martha told Liza, "Those birds look at the pickup loaded with barley." Liza ran towards the gentleman supervising the loading of grains. With an impish grin, she said, "The doves are hungry." The man smiled back, pulled beside a cattle feed trough, filled it with barley and kept it aside. The doves swooped down and it was a wonderful sight. In the frenzied quest, a dove got injured. Aunt and the little girl hurried to the injured creature. Martha leaned down, picked up the bird, brought it home, named it Peggy, lathered the wounded leg with antibiotic salve, put it in a wire-mesh cage and fed it with water and grain. Liza waited for Peggy to lay eggs. Day after day Liza went disappointed to find no eggs in the cage. On questioning about this, her aunt told her, "Peggy might lay eggs after her wound is cured and when we let go of her." One evening Liza's friend Dorey brought home a storm-damaged nest. The little girls lined it with a little wool and placed it inside Peggy's cage. To their amazement, Peggy climbed into it. "The bird loves it," smiled Dorey. Peggy's health seemed to improve and new feathers appeared on her. Another day, Liza tossed her schoolbag on to the sofa and ran to see Peggy. It wasn't there. Liza's sister Barbie had left the cage open after feeding Peggy. Liza ran out and saw Peggy perched on a mulberry bush. Hearing Liza Peggy flew back through the doorway and back into her cage, Liza, Barbie and Martha watched it with wonder. "We'll have to let her go. Peggy is grown and strong too," said Martha. Together they decided that Christmas Eve was the apt day to let Peggy join her friends. On Christmas Eve, Liza and Barbie brought home their friends to celebrate Peggy's freedom. The home was filled with the smell of baking cakes. Liza's mom whisked it from the oven and cut it into pieces. Peggy was fed too. With a loud Hip Hip Hooray, Martha opened the cage and out flew Peggy to the mulberry bush and sat there bewildered. Barbara ran out screaming, "Fly away Peggy, fly away." Peggy flew further away and away. And soon Peggy was nowhere in sight. Winter came to an end and there was no sign of Peggy anywhere around. But the cage stood open in its place.

It was spring season and every little thing in the garden came alive and so did memories of Peggy. One fine morning when everyone was still in bed Barbie called out, "come on everybody, we have a guest." There sat Peggy on the nest inside the cage proudly displaying the eggs she laid. Liza held out her hand full of grains and whispered, "Welcome home our love."

"Home beckons us with love."

□

Little Miss Idea

Every evening after study time Dayakanth and Suryakanth went to a park near their house. One evening the park was so crowded that the brothers never found an empty swing or see-saw or slide. As they walked around hand in hand, a colourful butterfly caught Dayakanth's attention. Soon the little boys were after that unusually coloured butterfly. It flew up and down, slow and fast and in circles too. At last it rested on a white chalk and the chalk turned multicoloured. The butterfly hovered around for a while and flew out of sight. The curious little boys picked up the chalk and walked back home talking excitedly about how it's possible for a butterfly to turn things colourful and if those flowers got their colours from butterflies. The very next evening they went upstairs and drew some pictures with that chalk. Bingo! Everything they drew turned out to be real and good. Thus, they managed to bring a swing, see-saw and slide on their terrace and played on them too. When the boys left the place the things also disappeared. The two brothers lived in their dream world happily for a while. The chalk grew smaller day after day and the boys began to worry.

Summer holidays were round the corner and the little boys eagerly awaited their little cousin sisters Lauren and Barbara to visit them. When they arrived Dayakanth and Suryakanth shared the good news to their little sisters and also the bad news that the chalk is growing smaller day by day. Barbara said thoughtfu ly, "wouldn't it be nice if you can draw that butterfly before the chalk becomes small enough to disappear?" So all four sat on the terrace and Dayakanth drew the butterfly that he and his brother saw that other evening. Oh yes! It was real and good. The butterfly fluttered its wings, hovered around those four little children and flew away. The children went after that colourful thing and again spotted another magic chalk. Dayakanth and Suryakanth felt so happy for their little sisters Lauren and Barbara. And at school the boys talked so proudly about little Barbara and nicknamed her as Little Miss Idea.

"Little sisters have big ideas."

□

Mango Orchard

James' orchard was a lovely place. Mani acted as the watchman who chased away monkeys from stealing yellow ripe bananas and his banana muffins. He was the proud owner of an air rifle and his brown spaniels did their bit to keep the monkeys, away. Whenever Mani saw a group of monkeys he pointed his rifle up at the sky and shot into the air to scare them away. James visited the orchard with his grand-daughters, Lauren and Barbara. The girls were pretty excited about the monkeys and they decided to make friends with those monkeys. They sat by a stream with a few mangoes in a basket. "Here you go," said Lauren throwing away a few ripe mangoes. The monkeys came closer to the girls and never missed a catch. This continued for days.

Mani told James, "I don't think I need the rifle anymore." James gave away a questioning look. Mani continued, "These monkeys don't steal mangoes. They just wait for me by the stream." Lauren interrupted excitedly, "And do you give them mangoes?" Mani nodded, "And so the monkeys never try to pluck mangoes from the trees. They even chase away the birds that peck at the fruits." Thus, Mani cared for the monkeys and they in turn cared for the orchard.

James looked confused and said, "It's amazing." Barbara decided to name the monkeys as Ram, Bubbly, Bunty, Cherry, Waldy and Jack. So, there were seven watchmen for the orchard. Mani was no longer an angry tired man. They took turns in watching over the orchard day and night. At night the monkeys sang aloud to ward off sleep:

We are monkeys
Living up on trees
We jump over the fences
And swing on branches
The bees and squirrels
Birds and spaniels
Just hate to watch us
Steal Mani's muffins
Mani has a gun
To us its fun
He shoots in the air
And we just don't dare
To steal yellow mangoes
That's too very mellow
Now we are friends with Mani
We guard the orchard triumphantly
We do not steal
Mangoes are our meal
For he shares them now
With lots of love.

"Sharing also means caring."

□

Mario, The Turtle

James, a 10-year-old boy loved animals and birds. He was studious too. Summer holidays meant a visit to his grandma's house. His grandma Wills lived in a village that was a few kilometers away from seashore. James always loved the annual gatherings at his grandma's house because he could meet his kith and kin and favourite cousins named Sam, Rajan and Justin. They had lots of fun spending time together at the seashore. They played beach volleyball. Spotting sea eagles and building sand castles were their pastime in addition to swimming. At home the popular games were dark room, hide and seek and carrom. Wills engaged the boys with stories of sea eagles killing her lambs. And some days the big boys kept watch for those deadly birds in the fields.

One day the boys brought home a wild caught turtle and named it Mario. Wills didn't approve of it. "Please take the turtle back to the sea," she said. James encountered looks of disapproval from some of his aunts. James retorted, "But it's not at all dangerous to have Mario at home." Nobody spoke. He continued, "Mario doesn't bark, need not be vaccinated or fed with costly pet food and taken for a daily walk." Justin walked in with a basket stuffed with bits of papers and said, "Mario can rest and sleep in this." When Wills warned James that the basket should not move from the working area into the house, James explained that the turtle needs nothing but the backyard water tank.

Every day the boys went fishing to a nearby pond and fed Mario with raw fish, snails and worms. One evening James cried out, "Hey boys, come here, it's magic." They saw James holding up Mario with its head outside the shell. Sam screeched, "It's wonderful." Their visits to the seashore came to an end as Mario became friendlier and neighbours started pouring in to have a look at the friendly turtle. Wills said in a stern tone, "These small children may trample upon Mario." And James sat watch. On seeing her grandsons' love for Mario, Wills was reminded of the story of Prince Ludwig II of Bavaria who had a pet tortoise.

The village kids talked about Mario as a tortoise. James and Justin showed them Mario's webbed feet and flat shell that helps it move easily through the water. Meanwhile, Rajan and Sam showed those children a picture of a tortoise and explained tortoises have round shells which animals can't bite and also rounded short feet to walk easily on land. Just then an intelligent kid blurted out, "So tortoises live on the land and turtles in water." James and his cousins chorused, "There you are kiddo! You got it right."

Summer holidays came to an end and it was time for James and it was time for the boys to leave. Wills didn't want to have Mario at home. "Mario will miss you and I'm too old to take efforts to feed it," clarified Wills. So, James and his cousins took Mario to the seashore and let it go. They stood there till Mario swam into the waters. They walked back home in silence. As the boys packed up their bags Justin whispered, "I'll miss Mario." Wills put her arms around the boys and said, "We shall sure have Mario back." Her eyes misted as she continued, "I'm too old to take care of Mario. That's why I let it go." James nodded and said, "Mario was reluctant to leave us. I gave it a gentle push."

After a year, the boys were back at the seashore with Wills calling out to Mario. One turtle swam to the shore. James jumped into the waters and picked it up. The turtle didn't pull its head into the shell. "It's Mario," screeched James. And all of them knew it was Mario. They spent another beautiful summer vacation with Mario.

"Not just elephants, even turtles have a steel-trap memory."

□

Neighbour's Dog

It was lunch interval. Lauren sat under a tamarind tree. Her friends sat around her in a circle. "Dad bought me a hutch," said Lauren. "A hutch?!," asked a puzzled Amy. "Yes," replied Lauren, "It's a wooden box with wire-netting in front." Kelly asked, "what do you do with a hutch?" Lauren sighed, "It's for my bunny. I want it to be safe from Caiser, my neighbour's dog." Kelly interrupted, "Yeah, dogs don't get along well with cats and bunnies." Lauren continued, "My bunny is white in colour with dense fur, long ears and red eyes. When I lift her up, she nibbles my nose."

"Oh, that's a loving animal," said Karen. Lauren said thoughtfully, "She doesn't love the hutch. She wants to move around freely." Kaushal thought for a while and said, "May be you should take her out of the hutch." Amy argued, "But what about Caiser?" Everyone was silent. "Caiser," Lauren said clenching her teeth, "I'll put him in his place." The bell rang and they ran to their classrooms. She liked Caiser but loved her bunny even more. When Lauren reached home, her dad said, "You look tired and worried, darling." Lauren looked at her dad, "It's about my bunny in a hutch." Prem consoled his daughter, "Lauren, your problem is solved." When they had finished dinner, the family sat round the fire. Lauren asked, "Are we going to lock up bunny in that hutch?" James too could read the sadness in his grand-daughter's eyes, "Yes my girl, for another day." Lauren felt delighted. "Really!"

Barbara said, "Mr. Newman and his family are moving away. And they are taking Caiser along with them." Lauren squealed with delight, ran into the kitchen and came out with a container. "What's that sis?," asked Barbara. "Baked mutton for Caiser," replied Lauren. Next evening Lauren, Barbara and James stood at their gate. "They are moving indeed," Lauren whispered. Mr. Newman came across the street, hugged Lauren, smiled and said, "Sorry, I knew you had a problem with Caiser. From today, your bunny will be safe." At school Lauren shared her happiness, "Caiser isn't in our neighbourhood and bunny is out of the hutch." A few days later, one evening, Mr. Newman greeted Lauren. "Little girl, how are you and your bunny?"

"Fine, thank you," replied Lauren. Mr. Newman walked back to his car and came with a brown coloured bunny. "Take this Lauren," he said. She carefully took the bunny aside and whispered, "You are very kind Mr. Newman. Thank you." Lauren felt so happy and so did her white-coloured bunny.

James shook hands with Mr. Newman, "This is a joy we had not expected." They waved goodbye and Lauren went to bed with her bunnies.

"A neighbour's pet may not be as kind as the neighbour."

□

Papaya Trees

Lauren and Barbara loved papayas for their colour and taste. "Papa why don't we grow trees that bear golden fruits?," asked Lauren showing off tiny round black papaya seeds that she had just taken out of the papaya she ate. Barbara said, "Wow! These seeds look like black pearls." Prem took those seeds in his hands, "sure darling we shall plant these seeds in our backyard." He dug a few small pits, put those seeds inside and covered it with sand. Monsoon came and went. Small saplings peeped out. "Here are our papaya trees," declared Barbara. Prem corrected his little girl, "These are saplings." The saplings soon became trees with flowers that turned into papayas. "But those papayas are green in colour," whined little Barbara. Prem and Lauren chuckled and Lauren said, "Dear, they are not yet ripened and that is why they are green in colour."

One morning the girls heard the chirping of birds in their backyard. "What's that chirping all about?," Prem wondered aloud. They went out and saw big yellow papayas. "Wow! Lets pluck them," whispered Barbara. And they enjoyed tasty papayas and shared them with their neighbours. That night Lauren dreamt of a smiling papaya tree that sang:

I'm a papaya tree
As you can see
Green and yellow papayas
For you and not for me
I sway but can't play around
I'm rooted to the ground
Little girls come pluck my fruits
Have your fill beside a brook
Do not climb on me
That won't make me happy
For I may bend and break
And you will have a fall.

Soon after Lauren and Barbara were busy chasing away birds that attempted to peck at the fruits.

"Fruit bearing trees never disappoint."

□

Pat and Strat

I'm the cat
I'm named Pat
By my mistress Betty
Who is a fatty

Festy is my kitten
She sleeps on Betty's mitten
Runs around the myrtle
And tease the panicky turtle

I hate Strat
A dirty rat
It makes me ratty
For it's a brat

Strat sips my milk
And makes me sulk
I give a chase
Its more than a steeplechase

It nibbles Betty's butter
Much to our anger

Strat made me a stalker
And the best runner

Strat, a little devil
Who always is marveled
To see me lose temper
And I dash off to a slumber.

"Cats and rats learn from each other."

□

Balloons are Fun

Lauren and Barbara loved to play with balloons. Lauren had a white balloon and she called it Pearl. Barbara loved purple and her balloon Polly floated alongside Pearl. They carried their balloons wherever they went. To the park, shop and fair but not to school. One day they went to a nearby fruit orchard. They plucked tasty red apples, had their fill and enjoyed playing. Friendly birds watched the girls play with Pearl and Polly. The balloons brushed against shiny red apples. A mynah tried its luck to peck Polly. Alas! Polly landed on Barbara's hands. A brightly coloured macaw took the red threads tied to Pearl and Polly in its beak and flew up. The girls squeaked with delight. It flew higher and dropped the thread. The balloons got stuck to the highest branch of a jack tree. Wind blew fiercely enough. But the balloons remained up there. The girls tried climbing up the jack tree but they couldn't reach for the highest branch. Lauren and Barbara waited for Pearl and Polly to float down, till sun set. They went home with a heavy heart. Barbara dreamt of a singing will-o'-the-wisp:

Pearl, a white balloon
Looked like the moon
It floated in the air
And soon found it's pair
Polly, a purple balloon
Joined Pearl so soon
They floated higher and higher
And became smaller and smaller
They got stuck
I tried my luck
To set them free
From the red apple tree
A monkey came swinging
A lion came roaring
A parrot sat chirping
A bear came growling
A cheetah came running
An owl sat hooting
They all sat looking
At those balloons flying
How do I get near!
For I fear
The animals around
Enjoying the flying balloons.

Next morning, soon after sunrise Lauren and Barbara ran to the orchard. Pearl and Polly were not to be seen. The girls sat down to munch on some carrots when they heard the cooing of a cuckoo. They looked up and saw a red-eyed cuckoo with a red beaked parrot beside it. From the parrot's beak dangled the red thread with Pearl and Polly. The girls sang:

Pearl and Polly are back
Lots of fun we pack
To make our summer holidays
The best of our days
Hey you cuckoo and parrot
Look! We munch on carrots
We are happy as can be
For both of you to see.

"Balloons are not just filled with air but loads of fun."

□

A Balloon knows no Boundaries

Pinky, a pink heart-shaped balloon, floated in the air. "What a beautiful world" she thought. The air was pure and cool wind drifted pinky further. Down below Pinky saw thick green covering a jungle. Pinky saw a pack of wolves eating up a dead calf. Pinky enjoyed the cool breeze atop the hills. Spotting Pinky a mother bear and a cub growled excitedly. Pinky swiftly moved down and rubbed past the cub's fluffy tail. The mother bear tried to catch Pinky. And "Whoosh!" Pinky was once again up in the sky. Pinky was careful about thorny trees and bushes. "If a thorn pricks me," thought Pinky, "that would be the end of my life." As Pinky moved across farms, farmers greeted her by waving their hands. Pinky swayed so gently and showered her love on the growing saplings. They grew up all of a sudden. "Here they are," cheered the farmers, "our tall and majestic mahogany trees." Soon Pinky was flying above a procession. She heard hooting and whistling. Amidst the street children, vagabonds, on lookers, idle-walkers and over enthusiastic women, Pinky saw an idol mounted on a decorated truck. "A religious procession," Pinky thought and hummed, "Oh Lord my God, When I in awesome wonder."

Pinky felt so cold on reaching a frozen continent. She dipped down. Few penguins were excited and played football. Pinky was simply tossed around. Finally, Pinky went up in the sky once again. It floated with pride and sang, "I'm on the top of the world looking down on creations." She floated higher and higher and tried to touch the sky. Pinky went up and up saying, "Yes, I can. Yes, I can." Minutes later Pinky heard a constant chant, "Yes, we can. Yes, we can." Pinky looked down to see thousands of people waving hands. She floated down and saw people hugging each other. She came further down and saw a smart man on the podium. That was Barack Obama. "These people are happy for this man," murmured Pinky. She brushed aside children who tried to snatch her. "Somebody would hug me too and I'll be gone," thought Pinky. She flew atop the podium and wished Obama the very best, "Its Obama's America." Pinky was sure that happiness was almost everywhere and flew away to see places and people.

"Let our minds float across the horizon like a balloon so light carrying no grudge, heaviness or worries and if possible reach the PROMISED LAND."

□

Majestic Queen

Queen, the black cat
Slept on a red ma
She woke up angry
I knew she was hungry

I threw some finger fish
Into her white dish
She ran to eat them up
One by one she gobbled up

Then she walked faster
Jumped so higher
Meowed so louder
Finally she woke up Berger

He looked around and yawned
Barked aloud and complained
That queen woke him up
And she is a boring muck

He strutted like a prince
Looked over the fence

And saw Queen the cat
Pouncing on a rat

Though Queen was smaller
She resembled a Tiger
That scared away Berger
He ran away farther.

"Cats and dogs just can't do without each other."
□

Raspberries

To Lauren and Barbara, raspberries meant an all-time favourite and hence wanted them in their vegetable garden. So, on that vacation, these two little girls started weeding their garden, dug holes for the seedlings and called out to their father, "Dad, we need help to plant the seedlings." Finally, the plants were in place to be watered and taken good care of. Honeybees became regular visitors for the nectar the flowers offered. Barbara nudged her mother, "Mom, what colour will be the raspberries, Red, black, white, orange, purple or golden yellow?" A sweet answer followed, "whatever is the colour, I promise you raspberry jam." Not a day passed without Barbara asking when the plants would give her fruits. And Lauren sang:

Oh my dear little sister
You can't be sweeter
When you ask for raspberries
But not those red cherries
You are just six, our tiny tot
One more year and you'll get lots

Of sweetest ripest raspberries
Jams, desserts, salads and smoothies
Be it A June-crop
Or ever-bearing crop
Happily, we shall pick cane berries
Tiny stickers are no worries
Freeze them and enjoy them
But, will you please stay mum?
Till we see the plants blossom!

Squirrels, rabbits, raccoons and one small fawn visited the garden daily to feed on raspberry plants. Barbara hated the wasps, beetles and plant bugs as she saw them biting into the raspberry leaves. Lauren just didn't find the time to shoo away the robins, blue jays and red-headed woodpeckers that tried pecking at the small fruits. Sounds made by the little girls did not seem to scare them away. So, their father came up with solution. He draped the bushes with nets and also engaged a gardener who made sure he spared the fruits for the girls. And they enjoyed finger licking good raspberries throughout.

"Raspberries can be a reason for making merry."

□

What We Sow, We Reap

Lot of reading on organic farming and ill-effects of pesticides prompted Lauren to pester uncle Jegan about helping her with a vegetable garden. Jegan himself being a not-so-good gardener went on to take some help from his wife Sylvia. So, aunt Sylvia stepped in to help Lauren with a vegetable patch. "We aren't depending on marketplace anymore," quipped Sylvia. "No chemicals no pesticides?," wondered Barbara aloud. Daddy Prem walked in with some expert advice, "vegetable beds should run north to south." Curious Lauren interrupted "Appa why not east to west?" Uncle Jegan, aunt Sylvia and Barbara sorted out seeds as dad Prem explained, "Darling, north to south because only then your plants get exposed to sunlight for long." Grannies Jeeva and Geetha made sure compost was ready. Aunt Sylvia chose greens such as fenugreek (methi), mustard (sason) and spinach. Lauren wanted to grow radishes, carrots and cabbage. Aunt Sylvia convinced little Lauren "but greens are quick growers." Months passed with the family putting in their efforts to grow seasonal vegetables. Little girls were too happy for their vegetable garden. Uncle Jegan sang:

Herbs are my favourite
Fresh tomatoes I take a bite
What's better than fresh vegetables
Radishes, carrots and cabbages
Their flavor and freshness
To eat them nieces make no fuss
Now it's time to party
With friends who are hungry
And family that's lovely.

Granny Jeeva talked about their vegetable patch during her evening walks with her friends and encouraged them to have their own gardens. In fact, she boasted "we never run out of vegetables at home." Another day uncle Jegan bragged about the freshness of vegetables and dad Prem winked at the little girls saying, "There's always a first time, so let's try a bountiful fruit garden too...."

"Planting seeds of goodness is a virtue."

□

Blushing Berries

There stood a flower with five white petals around a yellow stamen on a creeper. It then became a red berry with a green tinge and a peck of white. The red-bellied woodpecker tried to pick and devour at the berry. Little Barbara in a red frock and red cap sat beside the creeper all day to chase away the woodpecker. To Barbara, the berry looked edible and delicious. One night, when Barbara was asleep on her red cot, out from the soil came a black wriggly worm and nibbled at the berry. The very next morning on seeing the nibbled berry Barbara was worried. The friendly Robin flew aside to peek, "I will watch over the berry all nights if you would share it with me." That sounded like a good deal. And so, Barbara kept watch over by day and Robin by night. The berry grew firm and red. Not even a single speck of white and it looked ready to be plucked. "What do I name this?" thought Barbara. She called it the 'Blushing' berry as it stood so shy under the leaves. She took it to her mother to find if it was edible. Mom gave a nod. It was juicy, sweet and yummy. Half of the Blushing berry went into the refrigerator for Robin. The ever-grateful Robin gifted Barbara many of those Blushing berries strung together on a piece of straw. From then on, the blushing berry was named Strawberry.

"All berries that blush should turn red."

□

Sunrise Poem

It was early in the morning. Lauren woke up and saw a predawn grey. Barbara and Lauren decided to watch a rosebud bloom. Careful not to let the door slam, they stepped out. "Look at these dew-coloured leaves," whispered Lauren. Barbara managed to say a 'wow!'. They heard the cawing of crows and chirping of birds. "Hey Lauren!, look up the star fades," said Barbara. Breathing the chill air, they enjoyed watching the soft hues of dawn turn bright. "It's a new day," said Barbara. Lauren and Barbara raced upstairs to watch the sunrise. They saw a blue heron fly away in the distance. Lauren said softly, "All is still." Varied colours of rose, yellow and amber soared into the sky. "It's a beautiful and perfect sunrise," said Barbara. They felt the warmth of the early sun. All of a sudden, they looked at each other and ran down the staircase to their garden. The bud had already bloomed into a red rose. "Huh, we missed it again," said Barbara with a sigh. Lauren comforted her, "But there are many more buds." And the girls went back to curl beneath the blankets' warmth. Lauren hummed a song as she tried to catch some sleep.

Early in the morning
The sun is rising
With hues of colours
Into the sky they soar
The little girls clap
As the heron's wings flap
The star fades and
Let the brilliant shades
Pulsate in the sky
Up above the birds fly
Beautifully, the sun greets
But the world still sleeps
So, get up, get up, get up
To see the glorious sun rise up.

"Every sunrise marks a new beginning."

□

Big Dreamers Work Hard

It was swordplay, a game that dates to antiquity. Joel tall and upright in crimson tunic was in fact a serious fencer. Trained by his father Joseph, a former cadet world champion Joel started fencing when he was barely three. "Hungarians and Babylonians are the best when it comes to fencing," said Joseph. And Joel chuckled saying, "But you are the champion and I am talented." When Joel turned eight, he was sent off to be trained with elite fencers in Hungary. Though he missed his hometown Neyyoor, a sleepy yet beautiful place with sprawling British bungalows, meadows, a cute church with a church bell that was heard throughout the place and the river that flowed behind his home, Joel set his priorities right. He started to compete internationally. Though tradition was not on his side, Joel can't spell retreat. Sabre rattling became more than a passion to him.

As a child he dreamt of slicing body parts of his unprotected opponents like bacon. Then came the important event of his life. Years of training, hard work and commitment led Joel to the fencing floor. He walked into the arena carrying his weapon led by his attendant. Their eyes cast across the fencing floor. Joseph and his wife watched their son with pride and anticipation. Lights dimmed draping the arena in darkness except for spots that illuminated the action snooker style. Joel's opponent, a Hungarian with greater experience and advanced years made Joel feel tough. Fortune seeped towards the Hungarian. Joel fought hard and a few lightning strikes brought the scores level. Joel paused for a moment to steady the ship before the final assault. Joel anticipated his opponent's move. But fatally in a simultaneous lunge, the Hungarian's saber pierced Joel's defence. Though Joel saw it coming, he couldn't do much. He adjusted and countered but finally felt the weight of searching metal brush his body. The game was over. Years of preparation and focus gone on the turn of a blade! The Hungarian celebrated. Joel bogged down by disappointment reeled. His shoulders dropped and he shook his head. He gathered himself physically and offered his hand to the Hungarian because that was a civilized way to end a contest.

Minutes after Joel lost a battle, Joseph and Martha noticed a sparkle in his eyes that showed his determination. Joel hugged his mother and said, "Mama, I was almost good enough and I still love to fight." Martha loved her son that moment. She knew Joel was a fantastic and spectacular fencer and every spectator knew it. Joel believed the world appreciates dignity and determination. Today, he fences his best to win his next dream event, The Olympics.

"A battle is a battle, win or lose."

□

The Crow Was Never Black

Long ago there lived a crow. She was as white as milk and came out of her nest only at night to eat berries. One day she admired the night sky in its beauty. The crow was dumbstruck by the big round moon surrounded by twinkling stars. "The sky looks wonderful," thought the crow. From that night onwards the crow started to dream of the dark beautiful sky when she slept in the morning. Every night the crow sang a beautiful song:

You tiny star
You twinkle afar
Nearby the moon
You are my own
Every morning is a new day
And you fade away
I wait for the night
For you twinkle so bright.

And a twinkling star fell in love with her. The little star twinkled night after night. One night the crow decided to gift the star a diamond. So she began her flight towards a star with a diamond on her beak. Night passed by and the sun shone bright. The crow flew for hours. The crow neared the sun and he told her that she couldn't reach the star for the star is thousands of miles away. The crow scorned, "You jealous ball of fire, get away." The sun got angry and he scorched the crow's feathers. The sad crow with her scorched black feathers flew back to her nest. The sun set and the crow came out of her nest to greet her love, the star. She was so black that the star couldn't see her in the dark. The star broke down and disappeared behind the moon never to come out again. And the crow never slept in the morning but flew around in the hope of seeing her love. And that's why a crow caws, "A star, A star".

"A crow has a reason to caw."

□

The Kind Tree

It was a very hot summer. The jungle was as hot as hell and so was the old lion's den. There was a big shady redwood tree deep in the woods. Every afternoon the old lion came to rest under the tree. The lion looked hungry and weary. The tree felt so sad because all these years it had seen the lion strong and majestic. The tree asked, "Your majesty, are you hungry?" The hungry lion nodded, sighed and roared, "And tired too." The tree didn't want the lion to die of hunger.

That evening all the birds came to rest in their nests. The tree told them about the old lion and pitied him. "Dear vulture, I know you are strong and you eat flesh as the lion. Would you please drop a piece of flesh near the lion's den," requested the redwood tree. The vulture agreed to do so. Next afternoon the lion came limping to rest under the tree. "Dear Mr. Lion, the vulture would drop a big piece of flesh near you den," said the tree. "Everyday?!," roared an excited lion. The happy tree replied, "sure. The vulture is young, strong and kind-hearted too."

The next day the lion waited outside his den. Morning passed away. Afternoon was hot as usual.

The sun set and the lion went inside his den. The lion was sad and hungry. Just then he heard something fall outside. He saw a big piece of fresh meat. The lion looked up and saw the vulture fly round and round above the den. "Tasty meat," said the lion as he gobbled it up. The lion roared, "Thank you." The vulture cooed "You are welcome" and flew away. The lion thanked the tree. "Oh, it's always nice to be kind to others," said the tree. The wind blew and the tree swayed with happiness humming:

It's nice to be kind
So make up your mind
To help and to care
For friends in despair
It's never too late
For a leap of faith
Kindness and willingness
Are keys to happiness.

"An act of kindness is a feel-good factor."

□

The Lost Kitten

One spring day Juno and Leto set out in search of their lost kitten. They searched for it around their wooden cottage. "Have you found Pat?," asked Jerald from inside the cottage. "No daddy. Not yet," replied Juno from under a bush. The boys searched for Pat around hillocks, meadows and playgrounds. It was noon and they walked back home. Jerald and Bella felt bad about little Pat. After lunch they sat down to rest. "Did you look for Pat on that tall Oak tree behind the church?," asked Bella. The boys shook their heads.

In the evening, the boys walked down the street hand in hand towards the church. They peeped inside tree holes and under thick thorny bushes. Far away they heard dogs barking. On and on they went. Juno and Leto saw a pack of dogs under a mango tree. "Look up," screeched Leto pointing to a branch on his right. Both of them were happy to see Pat. "May be Pat is scared of dogs," whispered Juno. So, they chased away the dogs and tried to reach out to Pat. The kitten didn't know to climb down the tree. Juno went to his friend Vincent who lived nearby and borrowed a ladder. Vincent, Juno and

Leto rested the ladder on the mango tree. Vincent and Leto held it tight and Juno climbed up. With Pat on his shoulder Juno climbed down the ladder. The brothers thanked Vincent for his timely help. The family welcomed Pat with a song:

Our dear little kitten
I fried a chicken
To feed you tonight
Under the moonlight
And lovely little Pat
You grow up to be a wise cat.

Jerald made a wooden cage for their lovely kitten. And everyone waited for him to grow up.

"Every dumb little thing will grow up to be wise."

□

Velocar

It was a drowsy summer morning. Lauren went out in her red tiny car. "It's smaller than my bath tub," shouted little Barbara. Lauren smiled and said, "It's a two-seater car. Come, let's go for a drive." Barbara jumped in, "sure. That's nice Lauren."

"What's the name of this tiny roofless red car?," asked Barbara.

"Velocar," said Lauren. "It's our grandpa's."

Nadiya and Blossom were walking hand in hand. Velocar passed by. "Hey Lauren! Your tiny car looks cute." Blossom squealed. Lauren looked behind, stopped her car and said, "You may join us and tiny girls can sit on the fuel tank." Four of them drove along happily.

Lauren sang

This is my tiny car
A red old car
I call this velocar
We are set to go afar
Grandpa bought this model
From Charles Mochet stable.

Lauren enjoyed driving with her sister and friends. They stopped by a patch of a pretty garden. "Let's take a close look at these small flowering trees," said Barbara gleefully. Lauren followed her. Barbara said a rhyme:

We stopped by to see
styrax, halesia and fringe tree
In this beautiful garden
Amidst a fountain.

Blossom and Nadiya watered Shasta daisy and black-eyed susan.

Then they drove away. "It's fun to pass other vehicles," said Lauren. " And dozens upon dozens of people too," said Blossom. The traffic lights turned red. Lauren slammed on the brakes in her little red car that came to a screeching halt. "My God! we came bumper to bumper with that big Lorry," Barbara screeched. The traffic light turned green. "Here we go," said Lauren. So many scooters and motorcycles zoomed past the car. Soon there was a traffic jam. "Every driver is inching his way forward," shrugged Nadiya. "Where are the stop lights and traffic cops?," was Barbara's angry remark. Blossom moaned, "Oh, these blaring horns will make me deaf."

Lauren said, "Don't worry friends let's fly past." For the next few minutes, Velocar flew up in the air. "People are amazed. They are clicking photos," said Barbara looking down. Nadiya doubtfully questioned if Velocar could sail on waters and

Lauren nodded, "Of course darling. But today we are going back home."

On their way back, Lauren told them stories of her grandpa's escapades with the Velocar. And the little girls' adventure on road, water and air continued day after day.

"Little girls love big adventures."

□

Veggie Talk

In a vegetable garden, a potato and a carrot became good friends. They grew under the soil. Hence, they couldn't see each other but very much heard each other.

"Hey, golden tuber, howdy!" called out Gajar, the carrot.

Aalu, the potato said, "I'm fine and waiting to be dug out."

"Same here," mumbled Gajar.

'Thud, Thud, Thud' they heard footsteps. Out in the sunshine, Aalu and Gajar lay in a heap. Aalu took a look at Gajar and smiled, "hey dude, you look lean, lanky and fresh." Gajar slided towards Aalu from the top and whispered, "Hey spud, how do you taste like?" Aalu swirled around to say, "I taste earthy in a good way and creamy too. What about you fella?" Gajar rolled about and said, "Well, I taste sweet and nutty." Up came Motu, tied up the vegetables in a sack. "Plop," the sack landed in the marketplace. There came lovely Lauren, picked up a Gajar and sang:

Hey fleshy deeply coloured root

You are tastier than any fruit
Shredded raw carrots
An addition to salads
Carrot soup served hot
And juice served cold
I can't wait to take you home
You are savored in town.

Then came bubbly Barbie, picked up an Aalu and sang:

Brown round shaped spud
I love you baked and roasted
Ma loves you mashed
Pa loves you hashed
Lauren loves you crunchy
All in all, you are munchy.

Lauren and Barbie walked back home with few carrots and potatoes as much to Ma's and Pa's delight.

"Roots and tubers have less idea of life above soil."

□

Volcanoes

Pearl always woke up to the sound of rain falling, went about her daily work with the rain falling and when she went to bed, the last sound she heard was the rain falling. Rain was her constant companion. That night, Pearl hardly slept because the next day she was going on a visit to the Barren Island with her grand-daughters, Lauren and Barbara. As they packed up, Barbara questioned anxiously, "Do active volcanoes erupt fire always?" Pearl assured the little girls that everything is going to be fine. Lauren was too excited about using her newly acquired digital camera that she had learnt to use as well. Pearl, the little girls, their friends, few neighbours and the Krafft couple boarded a pleasure boat. Katia and Maurice Krafft were from France and they were crazy about filming and photographing active volcanoes. All of them have heard and read of volcanoes, so Katia and Maurice had not much news for the people on board. They were actually interested in seeing what an eruption would look like and smell like. Little children on board got busy looking for coral reefs and sea cucumbers. "Yeah, I spotted one, squealed Barbara. Lauren nonchalantly questioned, "Is it a fish?" A fat woman replied, "A sluggish creature. It's a delicacy in my home." The boat did a night cruise around the Barren Island and anchored off. Maurice Krafft announced, "We are almost 120 kms away from the volcano and safe." After two hours of wait, Lauren got to take some pictures of the glowing mouth. Volcanoes glowing by night seemed like a spectacular light show. Those sights simply dismissed grandmothers' stories of underground fire spitting dragons as mere stories.

On their way back, the entire crew and adventurists spend time looking at pictures and videos of erupting volcanoes. So many passenger ships, oil tankers and vessels passed by. 'Good Byes' from coastguard men cheered them up. The crew had enough stories about bats, birds like Megapod, Andaman Teal and Hawabill and Crabs of the Barren Island. Pearl laughed, "My goodness! The Barren Island isn't barren." That, feral goats were dropped in the island by a Station steamer from Port Blair and they surviving on sea water and cold springs left people in wonder. "But, what do they eat?," questioned a small boy. Lauren thought to herself that dropping those goats in such a hostile place is wickedness. Katie Krafft replied, "Probably, they eat the leaves of trees like Bukheri, Pathi and Jungli Jamun." They shared with each other their thoughts, fears, excitement, photos, videos and information about the volcanoes.

Back at home Lauren and Barbara drew pictures of long-necked feral goats reaching for tree leaves, flying foxes, rats, birds and crabs.

"Seek no garden in a barren land."

□

A Weekend to Remember

Lauren, her grandpa James, grandma Pearl and little sister Barbara planned a weekend getaway. Soon they all ended up in their quiet jungle house in the woods. Lauren woke up early and whispered, "Grandpa lets go out and enjoy the silent forests." James thought for a second and hesitatingly said "Darling, its dark outside." Lauren retorted, "Doesn't matter grandpa." Barbara came running along, "Let me join you." They stepped out silently. "Let's sit here at the base of this pine tree," said Lauren. Pearl joined them. Dawn appeared. Barbara said, "Look, now I can make out trees and shapes of rocks." A wild squirrel stared at Pearl, flicked its tail and ran away. Pearl remarked, "This pine tree must be 50 foot tall." They heard birds singing and knew the jungle was waking up.

Barbara stood up, "Look! a doe and her fawns."

Lauren gestured her sister to keep quiet, "Shhh, they move soundlessly." The little girls roamed around with James and Pearl. "A snake," screamed Lauren. It stood away from her. "Its aggressive and hissing," warned James. "We can't handle it.

Let's move away from it." They walked back to their jungle house. On the way they met cowboys. "Are you here to hunt cattle," asked Pearl. Sam, a lean young man replied, "we hunt bulls. They are as fierce as bears." James commented, "You enjoy wild freedom." The cowboys smiled and rode away in their horses.

The girls came across bright yellow flowers scattered around. "Wow! It looks like a gold carpet." Pearl smiled. Barbara felt happy. "It's good luck to walk over gold," she said. A cute fat pig ran across. An emu followed him. Barbara became curious. She asked, "Granny are they playing?" Pearl nodded, "May be." They saw a note that read "Don't run. Bears can run faster." Barbara looked so frightened and James comforted, "This is not a very dangerous place."

Pearl loved the giant beech trees and lacy cedars and James loved the leafy ferns and perky chickadee. Barbara loved to paint them, the chick-a-dee-dee-de of perky chickadee and they way the catch insects in the air. Lauren cherished the sounds of the jungle and called it 'The Wild Band'.

James exclaimed, "Hey girls come on, look at that flock of majestic geese flying low." Lauren hugged Pearl, "I can hear their busy conversations too." By nightfall, Pearl and Barbara declared, "We don't want to go to sleep." James gave away a questioning look, "Aren't you tired? Planning to enjoy the starry sky?" James and Barbara went off to sleep.

One thrilling day in a jungle and they waited for another dawn's early light. And they enjoyed a beautiful weekend with nature.

"A brush with the wild is all we need to appreciate it."

□

Weeny Bony Bunny

Small kit who lived in Bunny city was a fuzzy eater who just won't nibble on anything. Not grass, celery, cilantro, peppermint leaves, raspberry leaves, wheat grass, basil…nothing. Mother dam grew tired of complaining to father sire about baby kit's poor eating habits. So parents decided to send baby kit to a nibble nursery. At the nursery the kit learnt to nibble on everything edible and started enjoying its new nibbling habit. Baby kit grew up to be a cuddly bunny. Mother dam and father sire brought bunny back home. Alas! Once again bunny stopped nibbling on leaves but chewed on papers and pine cones. Cuddly bunny turned weeny and bony. Tired of parents' squeaking, weeny bony bunny decided to hop away. So…

Weeny bony bunny
Hopped away so funny
Nibbled away a carrot
Dropped by a parrot

Weeny bony bunny
Gave away a penny

Bought a white radish
And hopped away to Paris

Weeny bony bunny
Sipped a little honey
On a day that was sunny
And hopped off to see granny

Weeny bony bunny
Hopped into granny's pantry
Granny turned grumpy
About unruly bunny

Weeny bony bunny
Was no more weeny bony
He became a fatty
With a round tummy

Plump naughty bunny
Hopped into granny's winery
Saw a scary ratty
Hopped out so fiercely

Bunny stopped hopping
Simply started thinking
Of mommy and daddy
And hopped back to Bunny city.

"Even bunnies turn plump at their grandma's house."

□

Snowman

On a cold winter morning, Lauren woke up to see snowflakes outside her bedroom window. She was extremely fond of snow. So she ran towards the kitchen shouting, "Mama, its winter again." Lauren and her little sister Barbara spent their days sitting at windows watching snowfall. Very often Barbara remarked excitedly, "Its perfect greeting card scenery outside." Lauren's grandma Pearl was an interesting lady who told her stories of invisible snowmen who lived on trees covered with snow. Someday, Lauren and Barbara waited for hours trying to get a glimpse of snowmen who never existed in reality. Clasping Barbara's little hands, Papa Prem tried in vain to explain to her that snowmen were just imaginary creatures. Finally, they decided to make a snowman. Lauren, Barbara and Prem got into their jerkins, put on their gloves, mittens, brightly coloured Beanie caps and gumboots and went out into the snow. After two hours of thorough fun and work, a snowman stood in place. The little girls looked jubilant and ran around the snowman singing:

Hey you snowman
Grow as big as you can

You look round and chubby
With a white belly
Here, we hug you
Because we love you.

Later Lauren and Barbara helped their dad decorate the Christmas tree. In between Lauren rushed to see if the snowman remained in perfect shape. Every night after singing, 'Silent Night' the little girls went to bed and Papa Prem told them the story of the Christ child.

Christmas was so wonderful with get-togethers, sumptuous feasts, cheese, sausages, cakes and chocolates. For the girls it was even more special because they finally made a snowman and understood that snowmen existed only in stories. They sang their all time favourite song:

We made a frosty snowman
He is our wonder man
We dance and sing around him
And wonder what would make him
Dance along with us.

They talked to the snowman when no one was around. Every morning they took a shiny red apple to snowman saying, "It's a Christmas apple from America." Then Barbara would look into his eyes and scream, "why can't you open your mouth and talk?" On seeing it, Jegan, their uncle laughed aloud, "He can't talk darling. He is made of snow. No flesh, no blood, no bones, no brain and no life." With a beaming smile the girls would rush inside home. Christmas went by. The girls didn't seem to bother about the melting snowman for they knew how it was made and what it meant.

Few days later, Lauren clung to her mama's hand, pointed to the place where the snowman stood and sobbed "I miss that white cold plump fella." Prem hugged Lauren and murmured, "You know darling, we shall make a snow man in another eleven months."

School reopened after Christmas holidays and little girls counted the months to enjoy another Christmas, snowfall and snowman.

"A Christmas isn't complete without snow and fun."

□

Jai Ho Kalam Ji

We dare and dream, We are here to stay
With you, our adored leader
To see the dawn of an utopia
With our 'Target 3 Billion'
Your power of belief drives us so valiantly
We win our wars with missiles so revered

When you will be heard so loud
'The Family and The Nation' will unite
As one soul to reshape our destiny
Humanity will venture and soar with
'Wings of fire'
To fulfill what you spoke

'Ignited minds' will shine like the sun
And darkness too shall pass
The gift of an 'Indomitable Spirit'
Is what we all yearn, to behold
The 'Evolution of Enlightened Societies' and
'The Spirit of India' shine in its glory

The agni in your heart
Launch 'Inspiring Thoughts' which

Guide a million souls across this world
Also help them perceive 'Turning Points'
And 'The Life Tree' will stand complete
With purpose and dignity

Here we dream into the future
Without giving up hope, your dreams
We share to envision a powerful and just nation
Alongside a 'World Harmony Creator'
With 'The Luminous Sparks' leading us
To explore, the land, air and sea

No scum can muddy our hope
To push our way through and cope
The pangs of Mother India
And rejoice in the birth cry of India-2020
That would witness the end of scams.com
And beginning of 'What can I give'.com

Our journey will prolong, till we dream big
Achieve a sense of fulfillment
Worth, accomplishment and joy
We salute you Kalam Ji for
'You are born to blossom,' to spread your aura
Of grit, strength, reason and logic
Jai Hind!!!

"Don't just move when you are born to leap."

□□□